ONLY AT THE CHILDREN'S TABLE

Story by Daria Baron-Hall

Illustrations by Benton Mahan

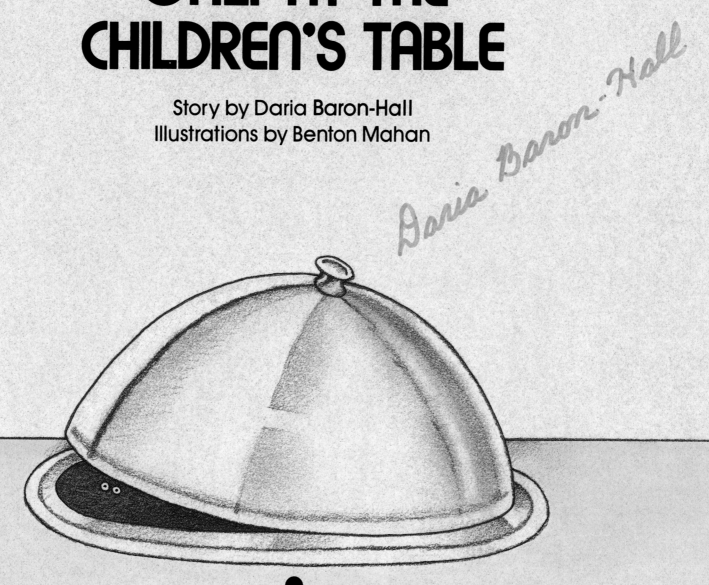

Daria Baron-Hall

Raintree Publishers

Milwaukee

For my mother, with love.
—D.B-H.

For Anna, Megan, and Kailey.
—B.M.

2 3 4 5 6 7 8 9 0   94 93 92 91 90

Library of Congress Number: 88-18585

Library of Congress Cataloging-in-Publication Data

Baron-Hall, Daria.
   Only at the children's table.

   Summary: During Christmas dinner a young girl who thinks she is too old to be sitting at the children's table discovers the special magic found only there.

   [1. Christmas—Fiction. 2. Dinners and dining—Fiction] I. Mahan, Ben, ill. II. Title.
PZ7.B268940n 1988 [E]   88-18585
ISBN 0-8172-2753-9 (lib. bdg.)

This year it was our turn to have the Christmas Eve dinner. We have lots of relatives. The whole family was invited, both sides. There were new cousins I hadn't seen before. And there were those who had grown a lot bigger. But none of them was my size. I was the oldest cousin by a lot.

Some of them were cute, and I liked to pick them up. Others needed to be told to settle down every few minutes. One liked our Christmas tree so much that he kept moving all the ornaments to different branches.

Another cousin wanted to water the tree over and over again. She filled the watering can up in the bathroom. Then she would pour water into the bowl until it overflowed. The carpet got all wet. But nobody was paying attention.

My mother and her sisters talked about Christmas when they were little. My father and his brothers discussed the stock market. Most of the other adults either listened or talked about their kids. Adults can have a good time together even if they aren't the same age.

Little kids like toys. My cousins were having a great time with toys I had outgrown years ago. I didn't even mind their playing with my old stuff. But they went all the way up to the attic to get them.

I generally keep old toys in my closet for a year or two—just in case I change my mind about them. When I know I'll never use them again, I put them in the attic.

13

It was getting close to dinner. I could smell the ham. The adult table looked beautiful. Mom had set out the good china with the Christmas design around the edges. She only used it once a year. There were red and green cloth napkins and crystal goblets, too. The silverware was from the good set.

Then there was the children's table. Actually, it was several card tables put together with one long plastic tablecloth. Mom said it was easier that way when one of the cousins spilled something. There were gaps where one card table was a little higher than the one adjoining it. When the cousins sat down, the children's table moved in different directions.

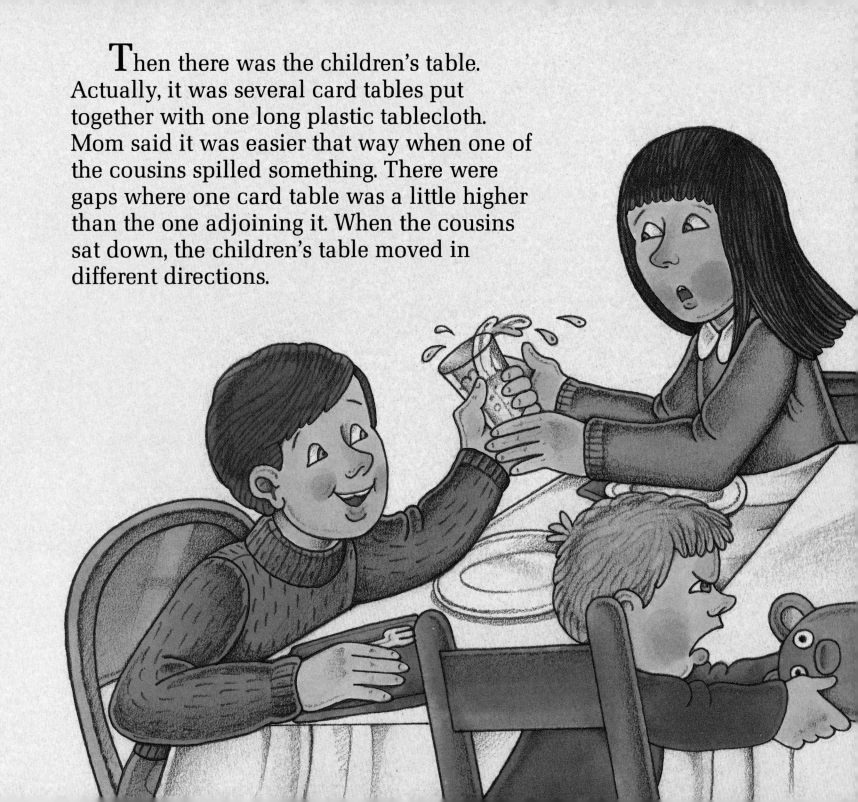

There weren't enough metal forks, so some kids had plastic ones from the supermarket. The plates were our everyday ones, but the napkins were Christmasy—even if they were paper.

It was almost time to sit down at the tables. I was sure that this year I could join the adults. There was an extra plate there. But just as I started to sit down, the doorbell rang.

It was Great-Aunt Bertha. She *never* came to Christmas dinner. She always stayed in Florida until Easter—except this year.

I helped Great-Aunt Bertha into my chair. And for me, it was back to the children's table, one more time.

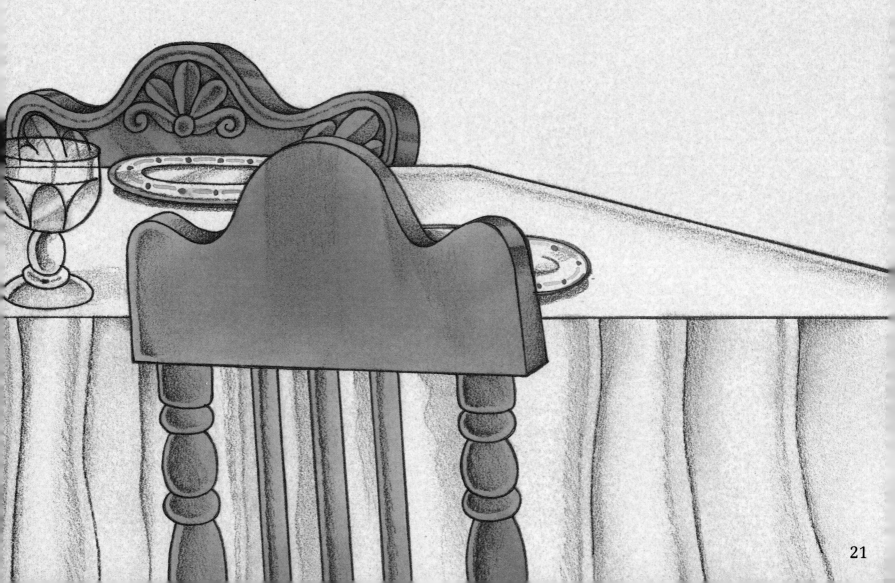

The good silver ham platter went to the adult table. I watched them pass it around.

I never saw who brought our covered ham platter. But as the oldest cousin, I pulled it closer and carefully lifted the lid. And there, sitting on the ham's juicy slices of fresh pineapple, were tiny elves. They slid down the sides of the ham before any of us could speak. They pleaded with us to be quiet and not tell our parents. No one at the adult table even noticed.

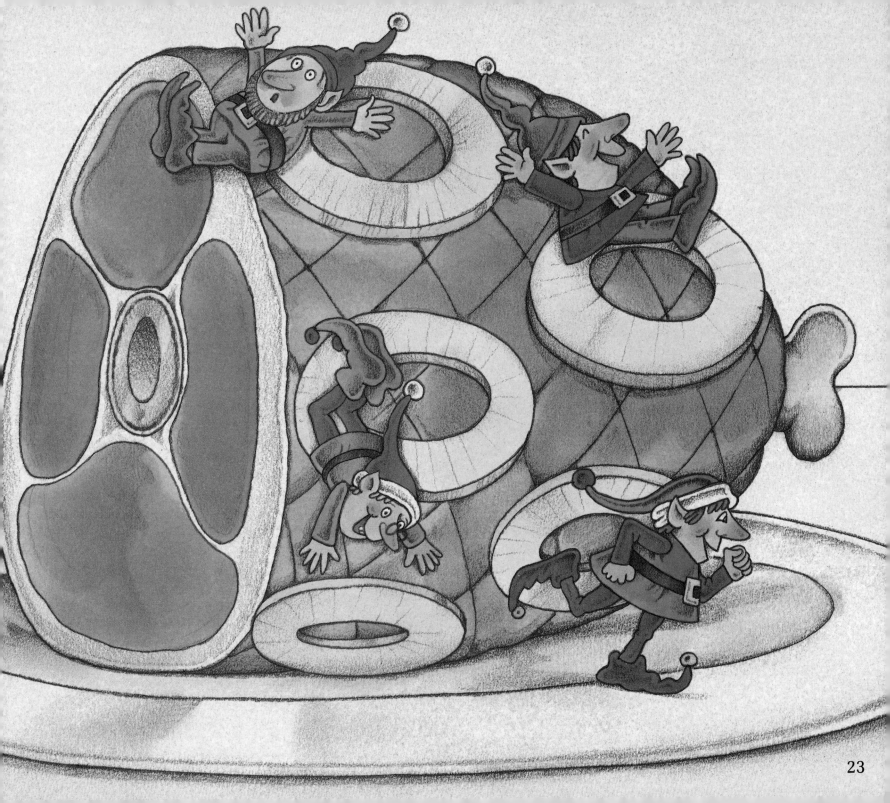

The elves ran over to each cousin, even the ones in high chairs! They took out tiny-sized paper and pencils and began asking each one of us what we wanted *most* for Christmas. They said that Santa wanted to get it right before we all grew up.

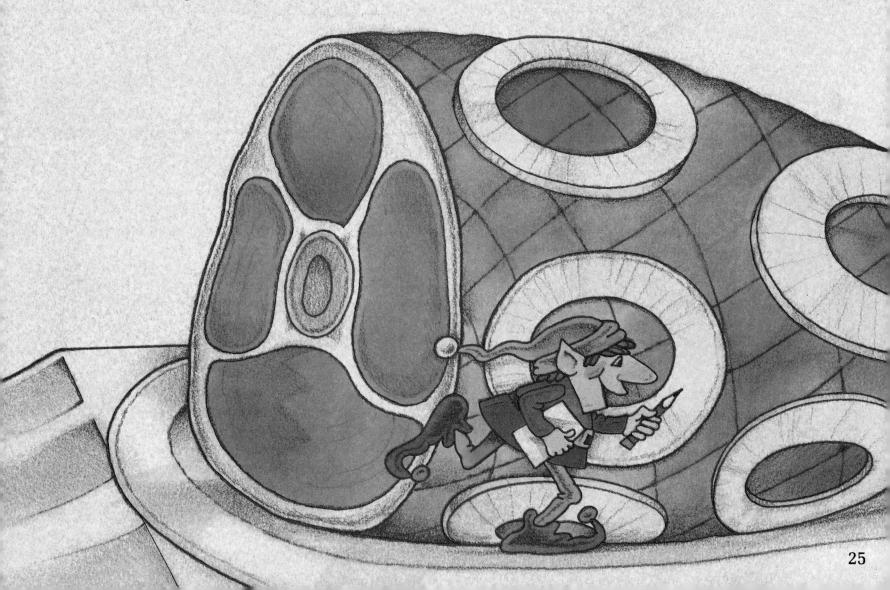

The very tallest elf came to me. He never took out his pencil and paper. I started to say something, but he waved both of his little hands at me. "Oh, I know what you want for Christmas," he said. "Next year you'll be there." He was pointing to the adult table.

It couldn't have been more than a moment before all the elves were gone. I do not know where they disappeared to. But not one cousin said a word to anybody at the other table.

It was during dessert that I realized just how special this Christmas dinner had been. Maybe the adult table was where I wanted to go, but the magic was only at the children's table.

Daria Baron-Hall was born in Jerusalem Israel, but she has lived in Port Allegany, Pennsylvania, for most of her life. She has a younger sister, Talia, who also has written a book.

Nineteen eighty-eight was Daria's year for winning contests. She was the Pennsylvania winner for the design of a Wish Book cover. Another piece of her work was shown on a network morning news show. A picture she designed is on display at the Children's Museum in Washington, D.C. And, for an essay Daria wrote, she won a microwave oven — which she gave to her father, who, she mentions, does the cooking at her house.

Daria's "most special day" was April 22,

1988. At a school assembly — which, of course, included Daria's English teacher and sponsor, Marcia Saiers, as well as her school librarian, Mary Palmer—she accepted her award for *Only at the Children's Table*. The

story was partly true and partly a product of Daria's imagination. It is true that Daria has many, many cousins, and it is definitely true that even though she is the oldest child, she is *still* sitting at the children's table.

The twenty honorable-mention winners in the **Raintree Publish-A-Book Contest** were: April Maria Burke, Old Town, Maine; Christine Debelak, Cleveland, Ohio; Aaron M. Eddy, Crossett, Arkansas; Tanisha Feacher, Homestead A.F.B., Florida; Brandon Geist, Schwenksville, Pennsylvania; Neal Kappenberg, North Bellmore, New York; Meegan Kelso, Coeur d'Alene, Idaho; Erin Mailath, Onalaska, Wisconsin; Olivia Julian Mendez, Richmond, California; Arnie Niekamp, Findlay, Ohio; Rebecca Papp, Hacienda Heights, California; Angela Rodrigues, San Lorenzo, California; Kirsten Ruckdeschel, Webster Groves, Missouri; Hannah Schneider, Washington, D.C.; Tres Sisson, Kaufman, Texas; Jenny Stalica, Buffalo, New York; Kenneth E. Stice, Des Arc, Arkansas; Kelley Tuggle, Largo, Florida; Regan Marie Valdes, Tampa, Florida; Scott Yoshikawa, San Jose, California.

Benton Mahan graduated from the Columbus College of Art and Design. He teaches art part-time and is the illustrator of many children's books. He is married and has two daughters. Mr. Mahan raises quarter horses and enjoys collecting antiques.